SCHOLASTIC

icky sticky readers

Deadly Dinosaurs

SCHOLASTIC INC.
New York Toronto London Auckland
Sydney Mexico City New Delhi Hong Kong

Dear family ∧ of new readers,
and friends

Welcome to Icky Sticky Readers, part of the Scholastic Reader program. At Scholast? we have taken over ninety years' worth of experience with teachers, parents, and children and put it into a program that is designed to match your child's interest an skills. Scholastic Readers are designed to support your child's efforts to learn how t read at every age and every stage.

LEVEL 1 READER
- Beginning Reader
- Preschool–Grade 1
- Sight words
- Words to sound out
- Simple sentences

LEVEL 2 READER
- Developing Reader
- Grades 1–2
- New vocabulary
- Longer sentences

LEVEL 3 READER
- Growing Reader
- Grades 1–3
- Reading for inspiration and information

For ideas about sharing books with your new reader, please visit www.scholastic.com. Enjoy helping your child learn to read and love to rea

Happy reading!

Francie Alexander
Chief Academic Officer
Scholastic Inc.

⚠ ICKY STICKY STICKERS

Every time you see this sign, look for a sticker to fill the space!

2

Contents

Copyright © 2015 by Scholastic Inc.

All rights reserved. Published by
Scholastic Inc., *Publishers since 1920.* SCHOLASTIC and associated
logos are trademarks and/or registered trademarks of Scholastic Inc.

No part of this publication may be reproduced, stored in a retrieval system,
or transmitted in any form or by any means, electronic, mechanical, photocopying,
recording, or otherwise, without written permission of the publisher. For information
regarding permission, write to Scholastic Inc., Attention: Permissions Department,
557 Broadway, New York, NY 10012.

ISBN 978-0-545-83347-9

12 11 10 9 8 7 6 5 4 3 2 1   15 16 17 18 19 20/0

Printed in the U.S.A.   40
First edition, August 2015

Scholastic is constantly working to lessen the environmental impact of our
manufacturing processes. To view our industry-leading paper procurement policy,
visit www.scholastic.com/paperpolicy.

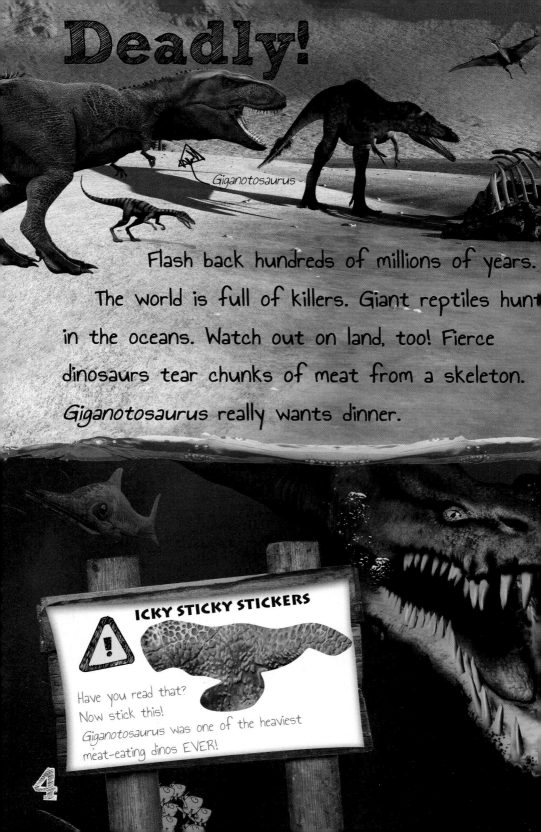

Deadly!

Giganotosaurus

Flash back hundreds of millions of years. The world is full of killers. Giant reptiles hunt in the oceans. Watch out on land, too! Fierce dinosaurs tear chunks of meat from a skeleton. *Giganotosaurus* really wants dinner.

ICKY STICKY STICKERS

Have you read that? Now stick this! Giganotosaurus was one of the heaviest meat-eating dinos EVER!

4

UH-OH!

fossil

t's a dinosaur fight!
t's a battle between
some of the deadliest
creatures ever.

Dino times

TRIASSIC

trye-AS-ik
The first small dinos lived
251–199 million years ago,
in the Triassic period.

JURASSIC
jur-AS-ik
Dinos got bigger and bigger
during the Jurassic period
(199–145 million years ago).

CRETACEOUS
kri-TAY-shuhs
By the Cretaceous period
(145–65 million years ago),
dinos came in all shapes
and sizes.

I'M A SPINE-CHILLING AMARGASAURUS.

Hundreds of different kinds of dinosaurs once roamed Earth. The deadliest ones had the WORST weapons. Horns that could make holes in other dinosaurs. Teeth that could crunch through bones as if they were potato chips. Every day could be a battle to the death.

Cryolophosaurus

YUP!

6

ICKY STICKY STICKERS

Have you read that?
Now stick this! *Troödon*
was smart—and it had razor-
sharp claws!

Velociraptor

Triceratops

DO YOU WANT A
PIECE OF ME?

Giant killers

Imagine seeing a 40-foot-long *Tyrannosaurus rex*! It's longer than your school bus, with gigantic jaws and 8-inch-long teeth! Stay very still. You'd better hope it doesn't like canned food!

MMM! KNOW WHERE I CAN BUY SOME KETCHUP?

TRY THE DINO-STORE!

8

Spinosaurus is even longer, and it's just as hungry. It can run twice as fast as you!

Tyrannosaurus rex

ICKY STICKY STICKERS

Have you read that? Now stick this! Spinosaurus's head was 6 feet long.

Don't worry—dinosaurs and humans never actually lived on Earth at the same time!

9

Tyrannosaurus rex and Spinosaurus were carnivores. Tyrannosaurus rex had powerful jaws with razor-sharp teeth, and it could bite with a force of 12,800 pounds. That's stronger than any other animal EVER!

UM . . . JUST WHAT DOES A GIANT T. REX EAT?

Monolophosaurus

ICKY STICKY STICKERS

Have you read that? Now stick this! T. rex bit really hard—harder than a fierce alligator does!

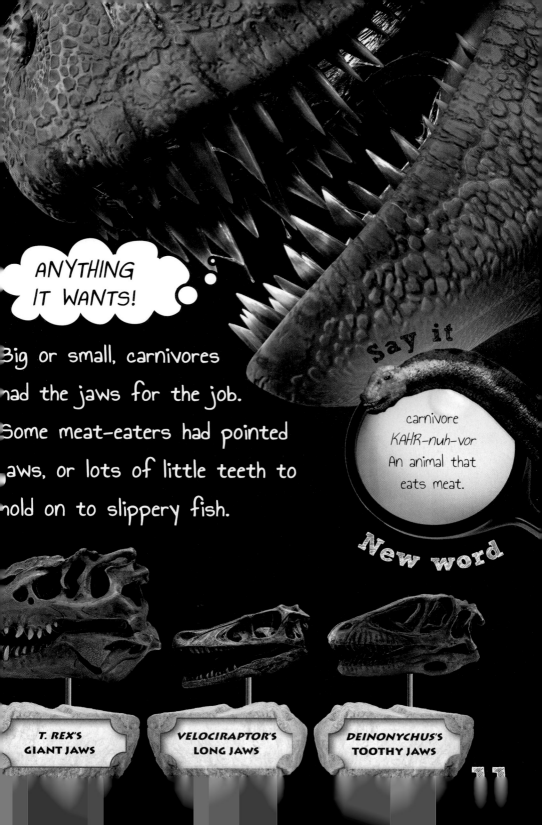

ANYTHING IT WANTS!

Big or small, carnivores had the jaws for the job. Some meat-eaters had pointed jaws, or lots of little teeth to hold on to slippery fish.

say it

carnivore
KAHR-nuh-vor
An animal that eats meat.

New word

T. REX'S GIANT JAWS

VELOCIRAPTOR'S LONG JAWS

DEINONYCHUS'S TOOTHY JAWS

NAILS DONE!

Meat-eaters could scratch as well as bite. They could REALLY scratch. Some dinosaurs, like *Megaraptor* and *Baryonyx*, had terrible

SAVAGE CLAWS!

Velociraptor claw

T. rex toe claw

Megaraptor claw

I DIDN'T CLAW MY WAY TO THE TOP OF THE FOOD CHAIN TO EAT SALAD!

Say it

Baryonyx claw

claw
klaw
A sharp, curved nail on an animal's foot.

10-inch-long claws on their "hands." Other dinosaurs, like *Utahraptor*, would grab victims, then use big toe claws to slash into their bellies.

New word

GULP!

Utahraptor claw

ICKY STICKY STICKERS

Have you read that? Now stick this! The name *Deinonychus* means "terrible claw."

Siats had a long, narrow skull. Its body was probably covered in feathers.

predator
PRED-uh-tur
An animal that hunts and eats other animals.

New word

Put it all together—size, power, jaws, and claws— and you get Siats. This 30-foot-long predator lived in North America over 98 million years ago. It was discovered in 2013 and named after a Native American monster that was said to snatch small children who wandered away.

Let's rumble!

The biggest bullies hunted in packs. They often attacked the youngest or weakest dinosaurs in a herd. That's how you get a quick, no-fuss meal. One predator would distract the victim so that it would leave the safety of its herd. Then the pack would close in for the kill. . . .

LIFE AND DEATH IN THE TIME OF THE DINOSAURS

1 This hungry *Velociraptor* and its pack are looking for a meal. Who will be their dinner?

2 Nearby, a *Protoceratops* mom realizes that her baby is missing. Oh, no!

ICKY STICKY STICKERS

Have you read that? Now stick this! *Velociraptor* stabbed its prey in the guts and let it bleed to death.

> I LIKE MY DINNER RAWR!

3 The baby *Protoceratops* has wandered away—a sad mistake.

4 The *Velociraptors* surround the young *Protoceratops*. Will Mom bring the herd in time to scare them off?

Meat-eaters weren't the only mean dinos. Some plant-eating dinosaurs were pretty deadly in a fight. They could stand up to meat-eaters or fight one another. *Triceratops* had monster horns 3 feet long!

The name *Triceratops* means "three-horned face." Three times the danger!

HORNS

Styracosaurus bashed its attackers with the big horns all over its head.

CLAWS

Therizinosaurus fought off predators with its 28-inch-long claws.

SPIKES

Iguanodon had spikes instead of thumbs. Very handy for self-defense!

AFTER YOU!

NO, AFTER YOU!

ICKY STICKY STICKERS

Have you read that? Now stick this! *Kosmoceratops* had up to 15 horns on its head!

Some dinosaurs had bony plates that acted as body armor. Even *T. rex* would find it tricky to bite through this tooth-breaking covering.

A swipe from an Ankylosaurus tail could cause a bad injury.

BANG!

ICKY STICKY STICKERS

Have you read that? Now stick this! *Stegosaurus* used its tail spikes to stab predators.

20

Some dinosaurs fought predators by hitting them with their tails. Ankylosaurus had a 100-pound club on its tail—great for smashing a hungry hunter.

Say it

club
kluhb
A thick, heavy object that is larger at one end.

New word

Whacking, whipping, stabbing—dinosaur tails were deadly weapons.

WHOOSH!

OOOF!

Food fight!

lizard

dinos ...

... and more dinos

fish

frogs

From fish to frogs, maggots to mammals—whatever the food, there was a dinosaur that loved to eat it. Some liked leafy greens. Some preferred a freshly killed dino steak. Others, called scavengers, ate the meat and bones of animals that were already dead.

small, furry mammals

WHAT'S MY FAVORITE NUMBER?

maggots

eggs

turtles

EIGHT! (ATE- GET IT?)

ICKY STICKY STICKERS

Have you read that? Now stick this! Every day, Carcharodontosaurus ate about 130 pounds of meat. That's like eating two nine-year-old kids a day!

23

Dinos disappear!

About 65 million years ago, something big happened. The dinosaurs suddenly died out. Most scientists think that a giant meteorite crashed into Earth. *BOOM!* The dinosaurs died—but they left behind clues about themselves.

say it!

New word

meteorite
MEE-tee-uh-rite
A piece of rock or metal from space that lands on Earth.

LOOKING A LITTLE UNDER THE WEATHER THERE, BUDDY.

⚠️ **ICKY STICKY STICKERS**

Have you read that? Now stick this! *Triceratops* was one of the last dinosaurs to roam the planet.

24

1 A giant meteorite crashes into Earth's surface.

2 The impact blows rocks and dust high into the sky.

3 Sunlight is blocked, and the weather gets colder—too cold for dinos!

GET IT? UNDER THE WEATHER?

Those clues are fossils, the remains of animals and plants that lived millions of years ago. The fossil clues can be bones, eggs, footprints . . . or even poop!

CAN YOU MATCH THE DINOSAUR TO THE FOSSIL?

Pachycephalosaurus

T. rex

BONES

EGGS

1 Look at the crest on the head of this skeleton.

2 These are fossilized eggs. Follow the trail to find their mom.

A poop fossil is called a coprolite (or should that be copro-HEAVY?!).

GROSS!

Oviraptor

Lambeosaurus

POOP

FOOTPRINTS

3 It takes a BIG dinosaur to make poop this size!

4 Who made this footprint? Follow the trail to see.

TOP 10 deadly dinos

So what was the deadliest dinosaur EVER? *Giganotosaurus* had a mouth big enough to fit an adult human inside. So did *Spinosaurus*. And it could swim. But *T. rex* had it all: strength, speed, and a 4-foot jaw filled with 60 blade-like teeth. RESPECT!

Spinosaurus

Tyrannosaurus rex

2

1

⚠️ **ICKY STICKY STICKERS**

Have you read that? Now stick this! *Carnotaurus* means "meat-eating bull."

THE KING IS HERE! GRR!

3

Giganotosaurus

Runners-up

4

Torvosaurus

5

Rajasaurus

6

Allosaurus

7

Tarbosaurus

8

Carcharodontosaurus

9

Carnotaurus

10

Ceratosaurus

Glossary

carnivore
An animal that eats meat.

claw
A sharp, curved nail on an animal's foot.

club
A thick, heavy object that is larger at one end.

dinosaur
A reptile, often very large, with four limbs and scaly or feathered skin. Dinosaurs laid eggs and lived on land. They died out 65 million years ago.

fossil
A bone, shell, footprint, or other trace of an animal or plant from millions of years ago, preserved as rock.

herd
A group of animals that live or travel together.

jaw
Either of the two bones that surround the mouth and hold the teeth in place.

meteorite
A piece of rock or metal from space that lands on Earth.

predator
An animal that hunts and eats other animals.

prey
An animal that is hunted and eaten by another animal

reptile
An animal with scaly skin that lays eggs. Snakes and crocodiles are reptiles, as were dinosaurs.

scavenger
An animal that eats dead animals that it did not kill.

skeleton
The set of bones that supports and protects an animal's body.

skull
The set of bones in the head.

Dino names

Allosaurus
AL-uh-SOR-uhs

Amargasaurus
ah-MAHR-guh-SOR-uhs

Ankylosaurus
ANG-kuh-luh-SOR-uhs

Argentinosaurus
AHR-juhn-TEE-nuh-SOR-uhs

Baryonyx
BAIR-ee-AHN-iks

Carcharodontosaurus
kahr-KAHR-oh-dahn-tuh-SOR-uhs

Carnotaurus
KAHR-nuh-TOR-uhs

Ceratosaurus
ser-AT-uh-SOR-uhs

Cryolophosaurus
KRYE-uh-loh-fuh-SOR-uhs

Deinonychus
dye-NAH-nik-uhs

Giganotosaurus
JEE-gan-oh-tuh-SOR-uhs

Iguanodon
ih-WAH-nuh-dahn

Kosmoceratops
kahz-muh-SER-uh-tahps

Lambeosaurus
LAM-bee-uh-SOR-uhs

Megaraptor
MEG-uh-RAP-tur

Monolophosaurus
MAHN-uh-loh-fuh-SOR-uhs

Oviraptor
OH-vuh-RAP-tur

Pachycephalosaurus
pak-ee-SEF-uh-luh-SOR-uhs

Protoceratops
proh-toh-SER-uh-tahps

Rajasaurus
RAH-juh-SOR-uhs

Siats
SEE-ahch

Spinosaurus
SPYE-noh-SOR-uhs

Stegosaurus
STEG-uh-SOR-uhs

Styracosaurus
stye-RAK-uh-SOR-uhs

Tarbosaurus
TAR-buh-SOR-uhs

Therizinosaurus
THER-uh-ZEE-nuh-SOR-uhs

Torvosaurus
TOR-vuh-SOR-uhs

Triceratops
trye-SER-uh-tahps

Troödon
TROH-uh-dahn

Tyrannosaurus rex
ti-RAN-uh-SOR-uhs reks

Utahraptor
YOO-tah-RAP-tur

Velociraptor
vuh-LAH-suh-RAP-tur

FIND OUT EGGS-ACTLY HOW TO SAY MY NAME!

31

Index

Image credits

32

n you find the right sticker for
each page? Read the dinosaur's
name, then find the page with
that name on it. Use the extra
stickers wherever you like!

Velociraptor

Spinosaurus

Troödon

T. rex

Triceratops

Deinonychus

Stegosaurus

Carcharodontosaurus

Carnotaurus

Giganotosaurus

Argentinosaurus